For Veronica and Rye Mepham
at the Rescuers Wildlife Sanctuary —S.C.

For Ethan —J.T.

tiger tales
an imprint of ME Media, LLC
202 Old Ridgefield Road, Wilton, CT 06897
Published in the United States 2005
Originally published in Great Britain 2005
By Little Tiger Press
An imprint of Magi Publications
Based on the title "Look Out for the Big Bad Fish!"
written by Sheridan Cain and illustrated by Tanya Linch
by Little Tiger Press
Text copyright ©2005 Little Tiger Press
Illustrations copyright ©2005 Jack Tickle
Library of Congress Cataloging-in-Publication Data
Cain, Sheridan.
The teeny weeny tadpole / by Sheridan Cain ; illustrated by Jack Tickle.
    p. cm.
Summary: Tadpole had been practicing jumping, and when he met Big
Fish he discovered he could jump all the way home.
ISBN 1-58925-047-8 (hardcover)
[1. Tadpoles—Fiction. 2. Jumping—Fiction.] I. Tickle, Jack, ill. II. Title.
PZ7.C1196Te 2005
[E]—dc22
                                                              2004017262
Printed in Singapore

The Teeny Weeny Tadpole

by Sheridan Cain

Illustrated by Jack Tickle

tiger tales

The Teeny Weeny Tadpole swam in
and out of the lily pads. Splish! Splash!
"Hello, my busy little tadpole," said
Mommy Frog. "It's such a nice day for
splashing and leaping…"

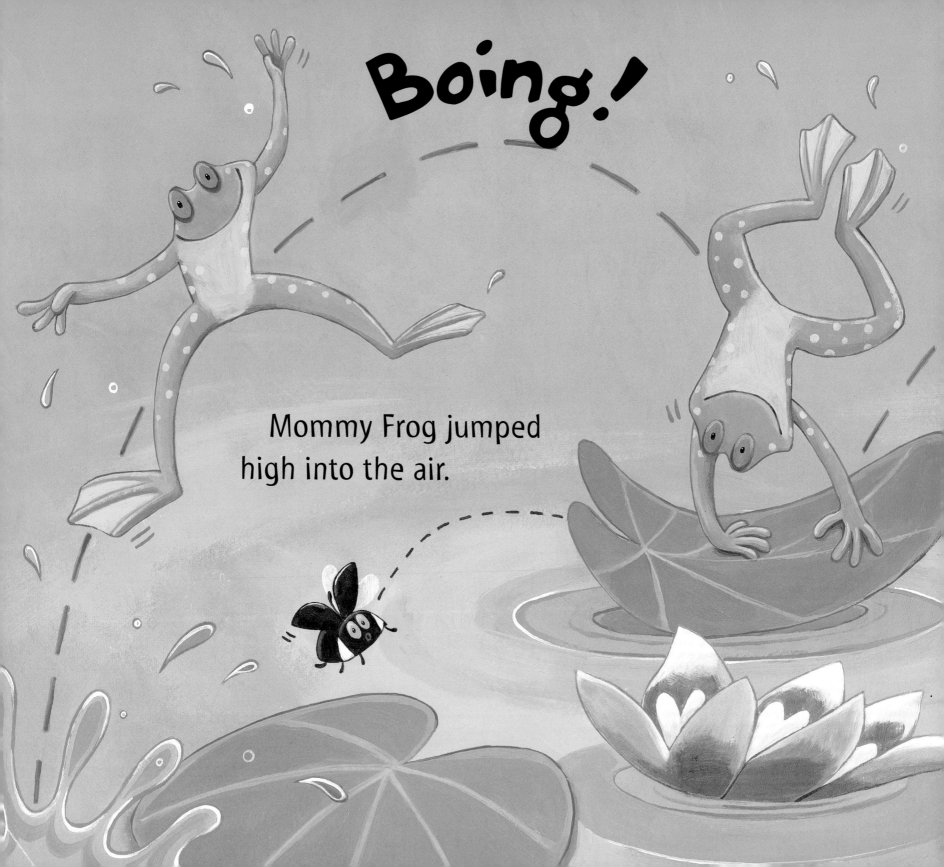

Boing!

Mommy Frog jumped
high into the air.

Flippity-flop!

She landed with a plop!
"I can do that!" said the Teeny
Weeny Tadpole, and he tried to leap
onto a lily pad. All he managed was
a splish and a splash.

"Mom, why can't I jump like you?" asked the Teeny Weeny Tadpole.
"Oh, you will, Tadpole," said Mommy Frog. "Just keep splishing and splashing."

The Teeny Weeny Tadpole swam off downstream. "Be careful, Tadpole," called Mommy Frog. "Look out for the Big Bad Fish!"

The Teeny Weeny Tadpole wiggled his way to the edge of the stream to splash among the water lilies. He looked up and saw a woolly face with a smudgy nose.

"Hello," said Tadpole. "Who are you?"

"I'm Lamb," said the woolly-faced animal.

"Can you jump?" asked Tadpole.

"You bet!" said Lamb. "Watch this!"

Boing!

Lamb jumped
high into the air.

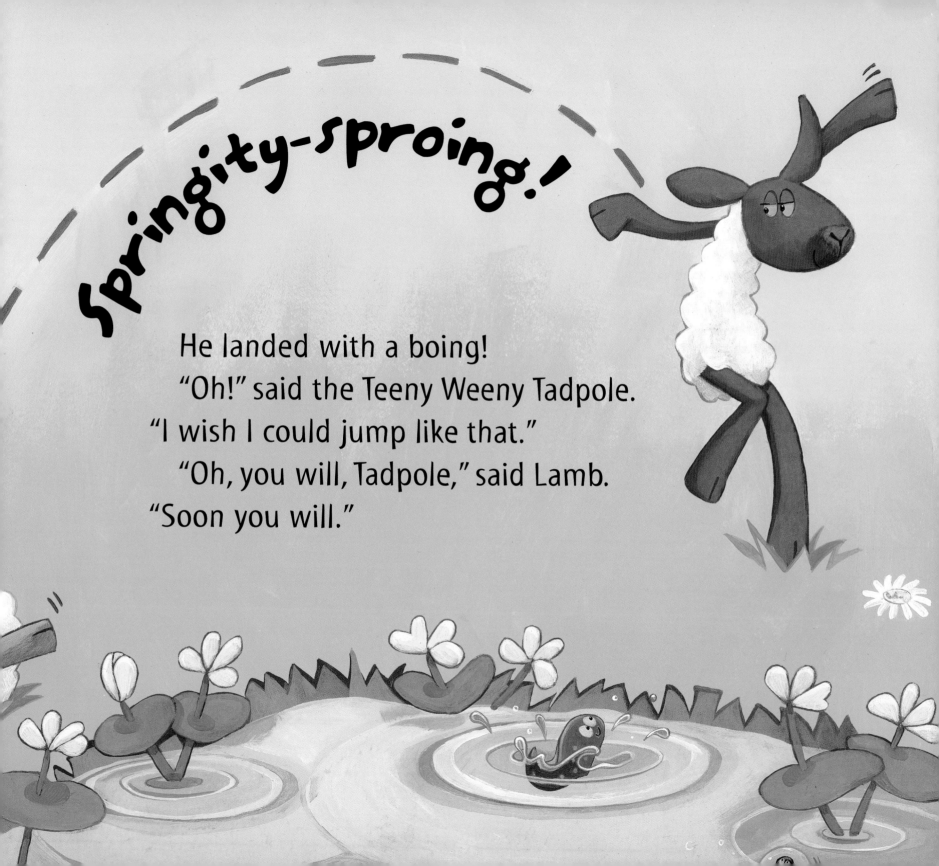

Springity-sproing!

He landed with a boing!
"Oh!" said the Teeny Weeny Tadpole.
"I wish I could jump like that."
"Oh, you will, Tadpole," said Lamb.
"Soon you will."

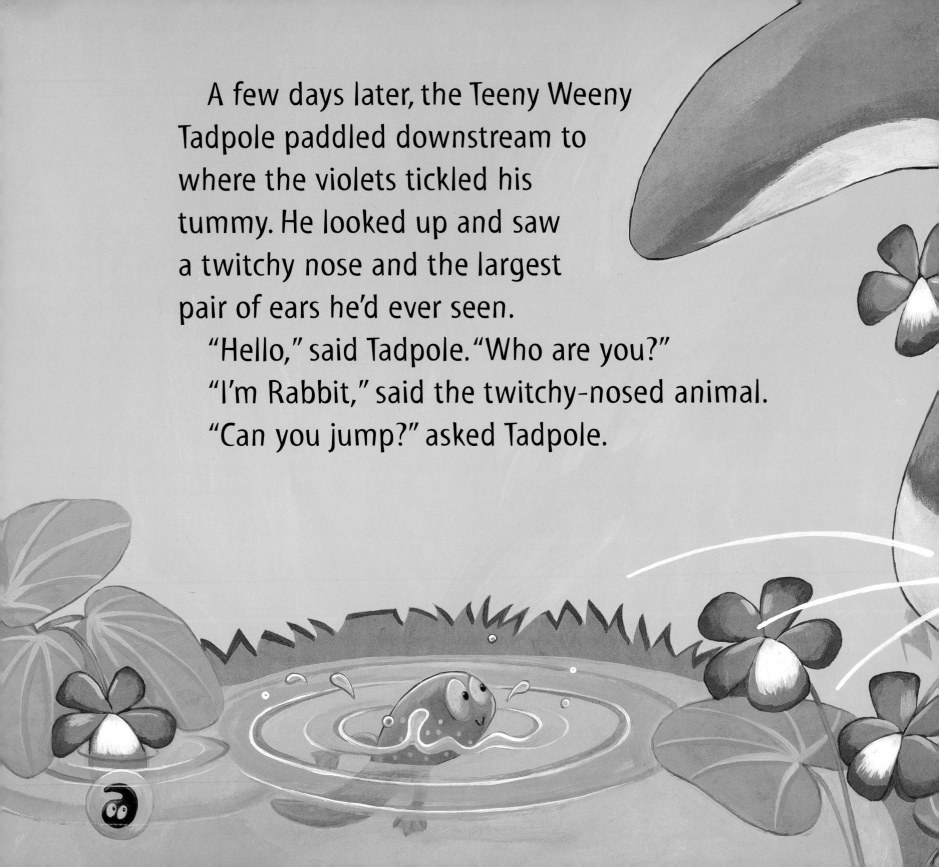

A few days later, the Teeny Weeny
Tadpole paddled downstream to
where the violets tickled his
tummy. He looked up and saw
a twitchy nose and the largest
pair of ears he'd ever seen.

"Hello," said Tadpole. "Who are you?"

"I'm Rabbit," said the twitchy-nosed animal.

"Can you jump?" asked Tadpole.

"Can I jump?" said Rabbit.
"Watch this!"

Boing!

Rabbit jumped high into the air.

Jumpity-jump!

Rabbit landed with a thump! "Wow," said the Teeny Weeny Tadpole. "I wish I could jump like that."

"Oh, you will, Tadpole," said Rabbit. "Very soon, you will."

Several days later, the Teeny Weeny Tadpole swam
out to where the tall grass waved in the wind. He saw
a pair of bug eyes and two springy legs.
"Hello," said Tadpole. "Who are you?"
"I'm Grasshopper," said the buggy-eyed creature.
"Can you jump?" asked Tadpole.

"Of course," said Grasshopper.
"Watch this!"

Grasshopper jumped
high into the air.

Hippity-hop!

Grasshopper landed with a bop!
"Whoa," said the Teeny Weeny
Tadpole. "I wish I could jump like that."
"Oh, you will, Tadpole," said
Grasshopper. "Very soon, you will."

The next time the Teeny Weeny Tadpole
went exploring, he swam far out to where
the stream widened and the water became
still. Tadpole looked down and saw a pair of
huge, rubbery lips.

"Hello," said Tadpole. "Who are you?"
"Hello," boomed the rubbery-lipped creature.
"I'm the Big Bad Fish, and

I EAT TADPOLES!"

The Big Bad Fish chased the Teeny Weeny Tadpole up…

and down…

and in and out
of the weeds...

getting
closer
and
closer
until...

Boing!

The Teeny Weeny Tadpole leaped high into the air, higher than Lamb, higher than Rabbit, and higher than Grasshopper. He leaped all the way home.

"Look, Mommy!" said Tadpole.
"I can jump just like you!"
His mother smiled proudly.
"Of course you can, my little FROG!"